John White Chadwick

**In Nazareth Town, a Christmas Fantasy**

And other Poems

John White Chadwick

**In Nazareth Town, a Christmas Fantasy**
*And other Poems*

ISBN/EAN: 9783743418158

Manufactured in Europe, USA, Canada, Australia, Japa

Cover: Foto ©Andreas Hilbeck / pixelio.de

Manufactured and distributed by brebook publishing software
(www.brebook.com)

John White Chadwick

**In Nazareth Town, a Christmas Fantasy**

# In Nazareth Town

## A Christmas Fantasy

## *AND OTHER POEMS*

BY

## JOHN W. CHADWICK
AUTHOR OF "A BOOK OF POEMS," ETC.

BOSTON

ROBERTS BROTHERS

1883

**Cambridge:**

PRINTED BY JOHN WILSON AND SON,

UNIVERSITY PRESS.

# CONTENTS.

|  |  | PAGE |
| --- | --- | --- |
| MARY | | 7 |
| IN NAZARETH TOWN | | 9 |
| LOST AND FOUND | | 16 |
| LITTLE HANNAH | | 18 |
| THE OLDEST STORY | | 21 |
| HEARD FROM | | 24 |
| MONADNOCK | | 25 |
| A WEDDING-SONG | | 26 |
| HIS MOTHER'S JOY | | 28 |
| TO JACOB ABBOTT | | 30 |
| IN DOG-DAYS | | 31 |
| IN AN UNKNOWN TONGUE | | 32 |
| LUCRETIA MOTT | | 36 |
| SNOW-MAIDENS | | 37 |
| "ALWAYS YOUNG FOR LIBERTY" | | 39 |
| HIS FORTUNE | | 40 |
| A DEDICATION | | 42 |
| MUGFORD'S VICTORY | | 43 |
| THE SILVER WEDDING | | 50 |
| IN THE WOOD | | 56 |

# 6 *CONTENTS.*

PAGE

AN ODE ON THE HUNDREDTH ANNIVERSARY OF CHAN-
NING'S BIRTH . . . . . . . . . . . . . . 61

UNDER THE SNOW . . . . . . . . . . . . 72

TO A. W. R. . . . . . . . . . . . . . 75

THE INEFFABLE NAME . . . . . . . . . . . 76

THE RISE OF MAN . . . . . . . . . . . . 77

THE MAN JESUS . . . . . . . . . . . . . 78

STARLIGHT . . . . . . . . . . . . . . 79

THE GOLDEN WEDDING . . . . . . . . . . . 80

THE GOOD SHIP " REGISTER " . . . . . . . . . 85

ANTI-DISCOURAGEMENT . . . . . . . . . . . 91

SEVEN TIMES ELEVEN . . . . . . . . . . . 96

JAN STEENER'S RIDE . . . . . . . . . . . 98

STORM AND SHINE . . . . . . . . . . . . 103

THE MEETING-HOUSE . . . . . . . . . . . . 105

JOHN WEISS . . . . . . . . . . . . . . 107

A SONNET FOR THE DAY . . . . . . . . . . 109

FATE . . . . . . . . . . . . . . . . 110

# MARY.

SINGING of one who bore this sweetest name
    Long, long ago, in bygone centuries,
Mother of One for whom our Christmas trees
    Are green and bright with never-ending fame,
I think of one whom HAVING seen we love,
    A mother Mary of these latter days, —
Mother and wife and friend whose simplest praise
    The memory of her meekness would reprove;
Who, bound long years, was patient in her pain,
    And still forgot her own in others' woe.
Blessing of blessings and immortal gain,
    Such grace as hers to so divinely know;
Daring believe that not His mother trod
    With whiter feet this highway of our God!

# IN NAZARETH TOWN.

A S to the rose's petals pure
   The rose's heart of gold,
Was Nazareth to the encircling hills
   In the brave days of old.

The narrow street, a straggling vine,
   Against the hillside clung ;
And from its stem the village homes
   In meagre clusters hung.

And down the street, with eager feet,
   The village mothers came :
Let fancy follow without fear,
   And listen void of blame.

A simple tale they have to tell,
 The bubbling spring beside :
The like doth come a thousand times
 By every time and tide.


No more than this, — enough of bliss
 For Mary, mother mild, —
Upon her breast there lies at rest
 A little new-born child.


O happy women at the well,
 For Mary's sake so glad,
Be tender with the tiny babe
 And with the growing lad !


Make sweet and pleasant to his feet
 The path while yet you may ;
For steep and rough it yet shall be
 For many a weary day.

The women climb the rugged street,
    And two there are that come
With pleasant chatter to the door
    Of good-man Joseph's home.


With them, unseen, we enter in :
    We see the humble state ;
The gentle mother, innocent
    Of all the impending fate.


How soft she sleeps, the blessed child
    Upon her bended arm !
How far away they seem to-day
    From all the things that harm !


O mother Mary, closer press
    Your baby to your heart !
There comes a day when nothing may
    Allay its cruel smart.

Those little feet have errands long
　　For God and man to go ;
Those little hands the chains must break
　　Of many a grinding woe.


That little piping voice shall wax
　　So terrible and strong,
That it shall shatter down the walls
　　Of many an ancient wrong.


O happy mother, were it thine
　　To see, as we can see,
All the fierce pain of heart and brain
　　That waits for him and thee, —


The wrath of men, the hate, the scorn,
　　The tried and tempted will,
The friends that falter and betray,
　　The enemies that kill, —

Would strength be thine to bear the load,
　To choose the fateful way
For him for whom thy life has gone
　In pledge this happy day?


We may not guess ; nor yet conceive
　Would joy or pain be thine,
If thou with prescient heart couldst all
　The coming years divine, —


Couldst see beyond the scourge and cross,
　Beyond the curse and shame,
Millenniums of godhead wait
　To crown his glorious name.

———————

Doth even now some vision come
　Of all the things to be,
That troubled looks across thy face
　Like conscious shadows flee?

Till thou dost start, and seem to cry :
　　" Oh, less and less of this !
Your God is not the man I bore,
　　Whose lips I dared to kiss."

———

Dear mother of the holy child,
　　Thy plea is not in vain :
Behold the God of centuries long
　　Becomes a man again !

Fade out the sophist's tangled schemes
　　As visions of the night ;
Breaks in the dawn of better things
　　As breaks the morning light.

O brother of the righteous will,
　　O brother full of grace !
Once more the human glory bathes
　　Thy grave and earnest face.

But all of this to thee is strange,
  As, safe from every harm,
Thou liest soft and warm and sweet
  Upon thy mother's arm.


And little dream the village folk,
  Upon the hillside brown,
What wondrous fame their Jesus' name
  Shall bring to Nazareth town.

December 25, 1882.

# LOST AND FOUND.

WHERE have they gone, the happy summer days,
  With all their loveliness of earth and sky,
  Which we have seen so gayly passing by,
Till now the last a moment more delays?

Whither have fled their mornings cool and sweet?
  Whither their dreamy haze of highest noon?
  Whither their sunset glories, and the croon
Of many waters murmurously fleet?

O friends, dear friends, who have been with me here,
  To-night, for all the miles that intervene,
  There is no inch of space our hearts between;
Come hark with me a voice of hope and cheer.

These summer days, that have so sweetly fled,
   Have their Avallon, wherein they abide,
   Like good King Arthur after he had died,
Or seemed to die, when still he was not dead.

It is a quiet place within the heart,
   Where they live on for many an after day,
   Blessing alike our labor and our play ;
And nevermore from us do they depart.

And when we know not why we are so gay,
   And when we laugh, nor know the reason why,
   God sees in us a gleam of summer sky,
Or hears some brook go laughing on its way.

And so in you I know God keeps for me
   The sweetness of the unreturning days,
   Safe from all harm and better than all praise :
Be mine, at least, such immortality.

   September 23, 1880.

# LITTLE HANNAH.

WHEN the earliest life of spring
First began to stir the sod,
And a blossom here and there
Softly sang the praise of God,

On a day of days there sprang,
Perfect from the dim unknown,
Such a flower as never yet
Had in field or meadow grown.

Yet indeed akin it was
To the blossoms, sweet and rare,
That in March their beauty bring
To the eager, waiting air.

Little sister did she seem
  Of the wind-flowers full of grace ;
Of the " Quaker-ladies " one,
  Or the arbutus' gentle race.


Cousin of the violets too,
  With their color in her eyes,
Greeting all the wonder new
  With a look of sweet surprise.


All the flowers that with her came,
  Had their hour and went away ;
But the little blue-eyed maid
  Tarried many a pleasant day.


Thrice the spring to summer grew,
  Thrice the merry autumn browned,
Thrice the winter whiteness fell
  Tenderly adown, around.

But before again the spring
　'Gan to softly shoot and stir,
Happy ways that she had known,
　Knew, alas, no more of her !

Gone the dainty little maid !
　Gone the blossom heavenly fair !
Gone, — but leaving all around
　Wondrous sweetness in the air.

Flowers are still her next of kin,
　Flowers that are so dainty sweet ;
Pansies are for thoughts of her,
　Roses for her gladness meet.

And in all her little world,
　If you can, the smallest spot
Find, that does not sweetly show
　Blossoms of forget-me-not.

January 28, 1883.

# THE OLDEST STORY.

UNDER the coverlet's snowy fold
    The tiniest stir that ever was seen,
And the tiniest sound, as if fairy folk
    Were cuddling under a leaf, I ween.

That is the baby: he came to town
    Only a day or two ago ;
But he looks as wise as if he knew
    All that a baby can ever know.

There he lies in a little heap,
    As soft as velvet, as warm as toast,
As rosy-red as the harvest moon
    Which I saw so big on the hazy coast.

Hear him gurgle and sputter and sigh,
    As if his dear little heart would break,
And scold away as if all the world
    Were only meant for his littleness' sake.


Blink, little eyes, at the strange new light;
    Hark, little ears, at the strange new sound:
Wonderful things shall you see and hear
    As the days and the months and the years go round.


Hardly you seem a Life at all;
    Only a Something with hands and feet,
Only a Feeling that things are warm,
    Only a Longing for something to eat.


Have you a thought in your downy head?
    Can you say to yourself so much as " I "?
Have you found out yet that you are yourself?
    Or has God what you will be by and by?

It 's only a little that we can guess,

    But it 's quite as much as we care to know ;

The rest will come with the fleeting years,

    Little by little, — and better so.


Enough for the day is the good thereof :

    The speck of a thing that is lying there,

And the presence that fills the silent house

    With the tender hush of a voiceless prayer.

October 29, 1877.

# HEARD FROM.

PLODDING a weary way, before untried,
    It chanced I came upon a group of men
  Busy about their work with eager ken.
I spoke to them of one who late had died, —
Knowing that he along this country-side
    Had toiled with such as these, o'er hill and fen ;
    Asked, had they known my friend ?  Oh, gladness
      when
Man after man with tender voice replied,
    And spoke his praise ; told of his earnest will,
The love which they had borne him deep and true,
    The generous passion of his noble skill,
Still doing well whate'er was his to do. .
    Again afoot, I said, " Pray God that I
    May so be *heard from* when I come to die."

Zoar, Mass., 1875.

# MONADNOCK.

THE merest bulge above the horizon's rim
  Of purplish blue, which you might think a cloud
  Low lying there, — that is Monadnock proud,
Full seventy miles away.   But far and dim
Although it be, I still can without glass
  Descry, as I were standing happy there
  Upon the topmost ledges gray and bare,
Something which with the shadows will not pass, —
A vision that abides : a fair young girl
  Lying her length ; her hair all disarrayed
    By the bold mountain-wind ; her cheeks aglow ;
As if that rocky summit should unfurl
  A rose of June !   And what if I had said,
    " Thrice fair Monadnock with her lying so ! "

CHESTERFIELD, August 24, 1879.

# A WEDDING–SONG.

I SAID : "My heart, now let us sing a song
    For a fair lady on her wedding-day ;
Some solemn hymn or pretty roundelay,
That shall be with her as she goes along
    To meet her joy, and for her happy feet
    Shall make a pleasant music, low and sweet."

Then said my heart : " It is right bold of thee
    To think that any song that we could sing
    Would for this lady be an offering
Meet for such gladness as hers needs must be,
    What time she goes to don her bridal ring,
    And her own heart makes sweetest carolling."

And so it is that with my lute unstrung,

   Lady, I come to greet thy wedding-day ;

   But once, methinks, I heard a poet say,

The sweetest songs remain for aye unsung.

   So mine, unsung, at thy dear feet I lay,

   And with a " Peace be with you ! " go my way.

October 8, 1879.

# HIS MOTHER'S JOY.

LITTLE, I ween, did Mary guess,
    As on her arm her baby lay,
What tides of joy would swell and beat,
    Through ages long, on Christmas day.

And what if she had known it all, —
    The awful splendor of his fame?
The inmost heart of all her joy
    Would still, methinks, have been the same :

The joy that every mother knows
    Who feels her babe against her breast :
The voyage long is overpast,
    And now is calm and peace and rest.

" Art thou the Christ?"   The wonder came

   As easy as her infant's breath :

But answer none.   Enough for her,

   That love had triumphed over death.

December 25, 1877.

# TO JACOB ABBOTT.

DEAR charmer of a thousand happy hours,
 My earliest guide into those blessed ways
Wherein I have delighted all my days,
Sweeter to me than laggard August showers
To thirsty fields, it was, to hear thee tell
 Of happy Rollo, and of Jonas wise,
 And Lucy with her meek inquiring eyes,
And all that happed to dearest Mary Bell.
Now thou art gone, so long the children's friend !
 But, as I muse, I seem at heaven's door
 To hear a sound which there I heard before,
When Danish Hans that way did softly wend, —
 A sound of children making merriest din
 Of welcome, as the old man enters in.

BROOKLYN, 1881.

# IN DOG–DAYS.

I SEE the landscape tremble in the heat,
    I hear the murmur of the rustling trees;
I close my eyes, and to myself I seem
    As one who floats mid odorous Indian seas.
Scarce draw the sails in the dull opiate air;
    Scarce stirs the breeze the opalescent calm;
Upon the sleeping islands that we pass,
    Scarce move the fringes of the shadowy palm.
And, as I sail, I seem to hear the voice
    Of one who reads some drowsy Eastern tale,
Telling of men untouched of all the ills
    Which for our hands and for our hearts prevail;
Ay, to be living in those days I seem,
And in those days still dreaming that I dream.

CHESTERFIELD, 1881.

# IN AN UNKNOWN TONGUE.

I KNOW full well what saith St. Paul;
  For unknown tongues he did not care;
It was as much as he could do
  To speak them good and fair.

Give him the known and understood;
  Five words of this he counted more
Than thousands ten of all the rest
  That men could babble o'er.

But then he did n't, as he might,
  Like Peter, take a wife about,
To tend his thorn, and soothe his heart,
  With combat wearied out.

And so he had no tiny Paul,
  No nonsense-prating, wee Pauline,
To make him half forget the strife
  His Jew and Greek between.


I cannot glory, as could he,
  In perils both by sea and land;
Of visions I have had a few, —
  Some hard to understand.


But I can glory in a Boy,
  As dear as ever poet sung;
And all his speech, from morn till eve,
  Is in an unknown tongue.


Strange, bubbling, rippling, gurgling sounds
  His pouting lips still overflow;
But what the meaning of them is,
  The wisest do not know.

3

Friends have I, learned in the Greek,
     In Latin, Hebrew, Spanish, Dutch,
In French and German ; and a few
     Of Sanscrit know — not much.


They come and hear the Baby's speech,
     As blithe as any song of bird ;
They wonder much, but go away,
     Nor understand a word.


It minds me now of mountain rills,
     And now of zigzag droning bees,
And now of sounds the summer makes
     Among the leafy trees.


And yet, if I should say the truth,
     Five words of his to me are more
Than of the words I understand
     Five hundred times a score.

For whatsoever they may mean
   To him, or to my learned friends,
One meaning, of all meanings best,
   He still to me commends :

That life is sweet for him and me,
   Though half its meaning be not guessed ;
That God is good, and I a child
   Upon his tender breast.

1878.

# LUCRETIA MOTT.

THRICE noble woman, who hast lived so long
    And served so well the people's sorest need !
Who still, howe'er thy heart might inly bleed,
Hast ever sung thy cheery household song ;
Turning from strenuous battle against wrong,
  With wholesome care thy growing flock to feed,
  In pastures green their frolic feet to lead,
To thee the laurel crown doth well belong ;
  For thou hast shown an unbelieving world,
Most womanly of women, that no less
  In the hot field where deadly shafts are hurled,
Women may keep their spirit's gentleness,
  Than when at home, in soft seclusion curled,
They live unmindful of the world's distress.

PHILADELPHIA, 1878.

# SNOW-MAIDENS.

A WINTER day upon the hill
    Where we our summer joyance took,
And all things to our pleasure bent
    As willows to a winding brook.


And there, upon the spot that knew
    Of baby joy and maiden grace,
Whirling about in ghostly dance,
    Are creatures of another race.


Tall, pale, and wonderfully fair,
    The chilly sunlight through them shines :
They dance with interwoven curves ;
    They move in wavy, mystic lines.

Weird sisterhood, your secret tell !
   Are ye the ghosts of vanished days, —
Of joys that will no more return,
   Of summers sweeter than all praise, —


Of hours when earth and heaven seemed
   To meet and touch and interblend,
And, face to face, we talked with God,
   As friend most dear with dearest friend?


O foolish heart, be not afraid.
   No plaint, but prophecy, is here ;
The spring shall come, and Life and Love
   Shall crown another golden year.

CHESTERFIELD, 1879.

# "ALWAYS YOUNG FOR LIBERTY."

CHANNING, when thou wast living among men,
  Thy pulse, that beat not always with the strong
  Full tide of health, when thou didst hear of wrong
O'erthrown, of freedom won, was once again
As quick and warm as in thy childhood, when
  Thou heard'st old ocean's mighty thunder-song
  Beating familiar cliffs and crags along ;
And thou didst glow as ardently as then.
Yes, thou wast always young for liberty ;
  And when a hundred years have passed away,
  Ay ! and a thousand from thy natal day,
Thy never dying spirit still shall be
  As young for Freedom as when here of old,
  In her great name, thou wast the boldest of the
    bold !

1880.

# HIS FORTUNE.

W. H. W.

IN the pleasant time of spring
　Came my noble friend to me,
Full of life as any leaf
　Budding on the orchard tree.

" I am going forth," he said,
　" Sailing down the busy world :
Fame and fortune I must make
　Ere again my sails are furled."

Comes the winter crisp and clear :
　What was that the message said?
Spring will come another year :
　Not for him, for he is — dead !

———————

Yes, thou hast made thy fortune, noble friend !

  We shall live on, and coax with weary toil

  Some scanty pittance from the grudging soil,

Or strain an aching back long years to tend

Sticks in the desert, striving still to mend

  Some social wrong, or with a few to moil

  For truths from which the many still recoil :

Long is the way and doubtful is the end.

But thou hast made thy fortuñe, found release

  From sordid care and every grief and pain ;

  Such things shall trouble thee no more again :

From every sorrow thine is sweet surcease.

  Sailing straight on across the unfathomed main,

Death hast thou found, and finding that is peace.

1879.

# A DEDICATION.

MY darling boy, kissed but a moment since,
       And laid away all rosy in the dark,
Is talking to himself.   What does he say?
Not much, in truth, that I can understand ;
But now and then, among the pretty sounds
That he is making, falls upon my ear
My name.   And then the sand-man softly comes
Upon him and he sleeps.

                         And what am I,
Here in my book, but as a little child
Trying to cheer the big and silent dark
With foolish words?   But listen, O my God,
*My* Father, and among them thou shalt hear
Thy name.   And soon I too shall sleep.
When I awake I shall be still with thee.

   1879.

# MUGFORD'S VICTORY.

Read in Marblehead, Mass., May 17, 1876, on the hundredth anniversary of the death of Captain James Mugford.

OUR mother, the pride of us all,
　　She sits on her crags by the shore,
And her feet they are wet with the waves
Whose foam is as flowers from the graves
　　Of her sons whom she welcomes no more,
And who answer no more to her call.


Amid weeds and sea-tangle and shells
　　They are buried far down in the deep, —
The deep which they loved to career.
　　Oh, might we awake them from sleep !
Oh, might they our voices but hear,
And the sound of our holiday bells !

Can it be she is thinking of them,

 Her face is so proud and so still,

And her lashes are moistened with tears?

Ho, little ones! pluck at her hem,

 Her lap with your jollity fill,

And ask of her thoughts and her fears.

 

" Fears!" — we have roused her at last;

 See! her lips part with a smile,

And laughter breaks forth from her eyes, —

" Fears! whence should they ever arise

 In our hearts, O my children, the while

We can remember the past?

 

" Can remember that morning of May,

 When Mugford went forth with his men,

Twenty, and all of them ours.

'Tis a hundred years to a day,

 And the sea and the shore are as then,

And as bright are the grass and the flowers;

 But our twenty — they come not again!

" He had heard of the terrible need
   Of the patriot army there
In Boston town.  Now for a deed
   To save it from despair !
To thrill with joy the great commander's heart,
And hope new-born to all the land impart !


" Hope ! ay ; that was the very name
Of the good ship that came
   From England far away,
Laden with enginery of death,
Food for the cannon's fiery breath ;
Hope-laden for great Washington,
Who, but for her, was quite undone
   A hundred years ago to-day.


" ' Oh, but to meet her there,
And grapple with her fair,
   Out in the open bay ! '
Mugford to Glover said.

How could he answer nay?
And Mugford sailed away,
Brave heart and newly wed.


" But what are woman's tears,
    And rosy cheeks made pale,
To one who far off hears
    The generations hail
A deed like this we celebrate to-day,
A hundred years since Mugford sailed away !


" I love to picture him,
Clear-eyed and strong of limb,
Gazing his last upon the rocky shore
His feet should press no more ;
Seeing the tall church-steeples fade away
In distance soft and gray ;
So dropping down below the horizon's rim
Where fame awaited him.

"Slow sailing from the east his victim came.

They met; brief parley; struggle brief and tame,

   And she was ours;

In Boston harbor safe ere set of sun,

Great joy for Washington!

   But heavy grew the hours

On Mugford's hands, longing to bring to me,

His mother proud, news of his victory;

But that was not to be!

"Abreast Nantasket's narrow strip of gray

The British cruisers lay:

They saw the daring skipper dropping down

From the much hated rebel-haunted town,

And in the twilight dim

Their boats awaited him,

While wind and tide conspired

To grant what they desired.

"Thickly they swarmed about his tiny craft;

But Mugford gayly laughed

And gave them blow for blow;

And many a hapless foe

Went hurtling down below.

    Upon the schooner's rail

    Fell, like a thresher's flail,

The strokes that beat the soul and sense apart,

And pistol-crack through many an eager heart

    Sent deadly hail.

But when the fight was o'er

Brave Mugford was no more.

    Crying, with death-white lip,

    ' Boys, don't give up the ship ! '

His soul struck out for heaven's peaceful shore.


    " We gave him burial meet ;

    Through every sobbing street

A thousand men marched with their arms reversed :

    And Parson Story told,

    In sentences of gold,

The tale since then a thousand times rehearsed."

Such is the story she tells,

    Our mother, the pride of us all.

Ring out your music, O bells,

    That ever such things could befall !

Ring not for Mugford alone,

Ring for the twenty unknown,

Who fought hand-to-hand at his side,

Who saw his last look when he died,

And who brought him, though dead, to his own !

# THE SILVER WEDDING.

## I.

THE stream and river bear a single name,
    Yet are they not the same.
    This hath the greater rest,
    And bears upon its breast
Vessels of deeper hold,
And freights more manifold.
The old is not the new, the new is not the old.

And you, dear hearts, are not the youthful pair,
To whom that day the whole world looked so fair ;
    When in the future's face
    You could no omen trace
Of aught you might not safely dare.

    The same, yet not the same,
    You have no word of blame

For any fate that hath befallen you,

> Howe'er, with fond regret,
>
> Your lashes may be wet

For stars withdrawn into the heavenly blue.


### II.

> BRIGHT was that morning hour,
>
> But, could you have the power,

Would you renew its rapture, sweet and fond ;

> Be now as you were then,
>
> For all the bitter pain

That makes the Here seem less than the Beyond?


> Life deepens as it goes ;
>
> The river seaward flows,

And as it flows there come from far away,

From out the heart of some mysterious day

That hath no night, but shineth on alway,

Yet other streams to swell the mystic tide,

And make it flow more strong and deep and wide,

Still holding gay and free

Their own identity,

As doth the Rhone what time it shoots amain

Through placid Leman's mountain-girded plain.


### III.

Sing, Muse, the happy day

When **I**, a stripling gay,

By happy fate and ordination led,

First in these faces dear their welcome read ;

Then heard the voices clear,

That grow each day more dear,

And felt their good right hands,

As strong as iron bands,

To hold me up in days of doubt and fear,

And brace my heart with friendship and good cheer.


Ay, merry were the days

When soft October's haze

Hung o'er the Island's various shifting scene,

And our good nag along the Serpentine

    Whirled us full fast !

    And merry were the nights

    With manifold delights

Of books and talk before the glowing fire ;

Nirvana's bliss, with nothing to desire

    But that these things might last.


## IV.

    DEAR hearts, how many years,

    How many hopes and fears,

Have come and gone since that dear morn of joy !

    What joy of summer weather

    Upon the hills together !

What joy of friends and books without alloy !


    How wide our feet have ranged,

    How many things have changed,

How many friends have fallen by the way !

 The Mothers full of grace ;

 The Boy whose earnest face

Kindled with larger promise every day !


 Dear Boy ! by what far shore,

 Thine earthly conflict o'er,

And all the struggle hard and small return,

 Wander thy tireless feet ?

 And what companions sweet

Assuage thy heart lest it too sorely yearn,

As ours for thee, till we God's patience learn ?


   V.

 But, friends, I do you wrong.

 Not such should be the song

That sings your silver wedding's dear delight.

 True hearts, when most bereft,

 Have countless treasures left ;

These should I sing, and bid you sing to-night.

Thanks for the vanished years,

With all their hopes and fears !

Ring ! silver bells, across the winter snow !

Ring out all care and fret,

Ring out all vain regret ;

Ring in the joy which only lovers know,

Lovers whose love is ripened as they go.


Ring ! happy silver bells !

Your merry clamor tells

Of love and joy and blessings manifold.

Draw nearer, each to each,

And say, with reverent speech,

" God give us grace to ring our bells of gold."

February 5, 1876.

# IN THE WOOD.

" MIDWAY upon the journey of our life
I found myself within a forest dim.

.        .        .        .        .

Ah me ! how hard a thing it is to say
What was this forest  .   .   .   .
But of the good to speak which there I found.
                                        DANTE, *Inferno*, Book I.

DEAR friend whom many a testing year
  Hath drawn unto my life more near,
Hath made unto my soul more dear !

My pen would thank thee, if it could,
For all the sweet and various good
Which thou hast done me in the wood ;

That mystic wood where on a day
Great Dante's feet had gone astray,
And Virgil met him in the way :

Its name is Life, and long had been
My stay among its brown and green
Ere first your happy tent was seen ;

And entering to your welcome free
I found a pleasant company,
And one as merry as could be.

Since then how many pleasant days,
Wandering along the forest ways,
We have been full of joy and praise.

What dear companions we have found,
Until where'er we look around
We cannot fail of holy ground.

For some that walked with us of yore
Have gone a little on before,
And we can speak with them no more.

Dark, dark the shadows now and then !
But sunshine ever comes again, —
The sunshine sweeter for the rain.


And even while with sorrow blind,
Our Mother Earth, so rarely kind,
Has blessed us in our heart and mind ;


Still showing us by day and night
A thousand visions of delight, —
The summer fields with daisies white,


The river winding through the hills,
The beauty everywhere that thrills
The heart until it overfills.


This have we known ; all this and more, —
The tug of thought, the pleasant lore
Of poets, and the gracious store

Of those for whom each beauteous thing
So in their hearts doth build and sing,
As robins in the later spring

In orchard trees ; whose blessed fate
It is God's world to recreate
And give to Beauty endless date.

Much have we found of sweet and good
While here together in the wood ;
And some things hardly understood.

But spite of sorrow and regret
I am so glad we came and met,
That some small space is left us yet

To clasp the moments fair and fleet,
To lie at Beauty's perfect feet,
To take the bitter with the sweet.

Late into heaven mayst thou return ;
Long may it be ere I must learn
To miss thee every way I turn.


Still keep for me a place apart
In the warm precincts of thy heart ;
Still be to me as now thou art, —


A light on every darkening way,
Thy hand in mine as on we stray,
Till solemn night succeeds the day.

December, 1880.

# AN ODE

FOR THE BROOKLYN CELEBRATION OF THE HUNDREDTH ANNI-
VERSARY OF CHANNING'S BIRTH, APRIL 7, 1880.

A HUNDRED years ago to-day!
　　How often in this latter time,
In fond memorial speech or rhyme,
Has it been ours these words to say!

A hundred years to-day, we said,
　　Since Concord bridge and Lexington
　　Saw the great struggle well begun
And the first heroes lying dead.

A hundred years since Bunker Hill
　　Saw the red-coated foemen reel
　　Once and again before the steel
Of Prescott's men, victorious still

In their defeat : a hundred years
   Since Independence bell rang out
   To all the people round about,
Who answered it with deafening cheers,


Proclaiming, spite the scorner's scorn,
   That then and there — the womb of Time
   Through sufferance triumphing sublime —
Another nation had been born.


" All men are equal in their birth,"
   Rang out the steeple-rocking bell :
   Rejoice, O heaven !   Give heed, O hell !
Here *was* good news to all the earth.


And still our hearts have kept the count
   Of things that daily brought more near,
   Through various hap of hope or fear,
The pattern visioned in the Mount.

Nor yet the tale is fully told
    Of all the years that brought us pain,
    And through the age of iron again
The dawning of the age of gold.

---

But naught of this has brought us here,
    With the old saying on our lips,
    What time the rolling planet dips
Into the spring-tide of the year.

Apart from all the dire alarms
    Of field and flood in that old time,
    With reverent feet our fancies climb
To where a mother's circling arms

Enraptured hold a babe new born ;
    And who was there to prophesy,
    Though loving hearts beat strong and high,
Of what a day this was the morn ?

For in that life but just begun
  The prescient fates a gift had bound,
  As dear to man as any found
Within the courses of the sun.


A gift of manhood strong and wise,
  Nor foreign to the lowliest earth,
  Whereon the Word has human birth,
Howe'er conversant with the skies.

———


A hundred years ago to-day,
  Since Channing's individual life
  From out the depths of being, rife
With spiritual essence, found a way,


And welcome here, and forces kind
  To gently nurse his growing power
  With steady help until the flower
Of instinct was a conscious mind.

To him the sea its message brought,
  Filling his mind with sacred awe,
  What time his eye enraptured saw
Its wildest tumult, or he caught

From its deep calm some peace of heart.
  To him the ages brought their lore
  Of books, and living men their store
Of thought; and still the better part

Of all his nurture was the eye
  Turned inward, seeking in the mind
  Some higher, deeper law to find
Than that which spheres the starry sky.

———

And so the youth to manhood came:
  A being frail, — with nameless eyes,
  That seemed to look on Paradise, —
As clear as dew, as clean as flame.

5

He willed in quiet to abide,
  Leading his flock through pastures green,
  And by the waters still, where lean
The mystic trees on either side.


But on his listening ear there fell
  The jarring discord of the sects,
  Still making, with their war of texts,
The pleasant earth a kind of hell.


He saw the Father's sacred name
  Made dim by Calvary's suffering rood ;
  Man devil-born, — a spawning flood,
Engendering naught but curse and shame.


He saw the freedom of the mind
  Denied, and doubt esteemed a crime, —
  The path whereby the boldest climb
To heights which cowards never find.

He saw the manhood which to him
　　Was image of the highest God
　　Trodden, as if it were a clod,
'Neath slavery's idol-chariot grim.


He saw it fouled with various sin,
　　Sick'ning from lack of air and light,
　　Abjuring glories infinite
To fatten at the sensual bin.


He heard and saw : his shepherd's rod
　　With grieving heart he broke in twain ;
　　The wondering world beheld again
A prophet of the living God.


Then, as of old, was heard a voice :
　　" His way prepare," and, " Come with me,
　　All ye that heavy-laden be ;
Take up *my* burden and rejoice ! "

It rang through all the sleepy land
In tones so sweet and silver clear,
The waking people seemed to hear
The accents of divine command.


The statesman heard it in his place ;
The oppressor in his cursèd field ;
And hearts beyond the ocean yield
Allegiance to his truth and grace.


Our Father, God ; our Brother, man, —
On these commandments twain he hung
The law and prophets all ; and rung —
For all the churches' eager ban —


A hundred changes deep and strong ;
Let who would hear him or forbear,
The ancient lie he would not spare,
The doubtful right, the vested wrong.

What words were his of purest flame,
  When, straining up from height to height,
  He felt the Presence infinite,
And named the Everlasting Name?

With him the thought and deed were one:
  Man was indeed the Son of God;
  "What, strike a man!" *   Break every rod
Of hate beneath the all-seeing sun.

So greatly born, how dare to trail
  Our festal garlands in the mire!
  How dare *not* evermore aspire
To Him who is within the veil!

———

In weakness made each day more strong,
  Softly his days went trooping past,
  Till robed in beauty came the last,
And with the sun he went along:

* His argument against flogging in the navy.

Not to oblivion's dreamless sleep,
But, like the sun, on other lands
To shine, where other busier hands
The fields immortal sow and reap.

———————

And he is ours !   Yes, if we dare,
Leaving the letter of his creed,
Say to his mighty spirit, " Lead ;
We follow hard ; " — yes, if no care

Is ours for aught but this : to know
What is God's truth, and knowing this
To count it still our dearest bliss
To go with that where'er it go.

So shall we go with him ; so feel
That comfort which the Spirit of Truth
Gives all who with his loving ruth
Are pledged to her for woe or weal.

———————

O thou whom, though we have not seen,
  We love ! upon our toilsome way
  Be thy pure spirit as a ray
From out that Light which is too clean


Uncleanness to behold ; shine clear,
  That to our dimly peering eyes
  All hidden truths, all specious lies,
That which they are may straight appear.


There is no ending to thy road,
  No limit to thy fleeting goal,
  But speeds the ever-greatening soul
From truth to truth, from God to God.

# UNDER THE SNOW.

DEEP under snow the mountain world
    For many a week had lain ;
Deep in my heart for many a year
    Had hid its viewless pain.

There came a day of warmer sun
    From out the winter sky,
And premonitions of the spring
    Went wandering softly by.

And lo, a bit of earth revealed !
    And lo, at little feet
Pressing the cold and cheerless sod,
    One pansy, pure and sweet !

" Pansies for thoughts ! " and oh, for me
    This pansy of the snow
Has thoughts that deeper than the depths
    Of mountain bases go, —

Thoughts of my little baby flower
    Beneath the mounded sod ;
Thoughts of the baby life that lives
    Forevermore with God.

Oh, gently falls the glistening snow
    Where he so long has lain !
Oh, gently fall the years of God
    Upon my bitter pain !

Fall deeper yet, O years of God !
    There comes another day
When winds from off the hills beyond
    Shall melt your snows away,

And many a dear, long-hidden thing
    Shall then be brought to light ;
And then who knows but my lost Face
    Shall bloom again as bright


As this wee blossom, hid so long,
    But waiting tenderly
Till it could bring to me a thought
    Of Immortality !

February 12, 1881.

# TO A. W. R.

ON READING HER BOOK OF POEMS CALLED "THE RING OF
AMETHYST."

I T came to me one perfect summer day
   Amid the tender beauty of the hills,
   Whose every niche a poet's memory fills
With echoes of his own resounding lay.
Died out the children's voices at their play,
   While sweet for me as lapse of mountain rills,
   Or fragrance that some rose's heart distils,
Your gentle verses had with me their way.
I read and read : the scene was all forgot ;
   Down dropped the sun above the poet's home ;
   The first faint stars came out in heaven's dome ;
Alone with you, all other things were not ;
   Till sudden, pausing, lo, the purple mist
   Had made the hills *a ring of amethyst !*

CHESTERFIELD, July 5, 1878.

# THE INEFFABLE NAME.

I SEE an angel with dilated eyes
    Filled with a wonder sweet beyond compare,
  Around whose brows her wind-blown golden hair
Makes aureole splendor, and her finger lies
Upon her lips.   Dear angel of surprise,
    The symbol thou of spirits high and fair,
    Who to be silent still serenely dare,
Before all wonders of the earth and skies.
How name aright the Power that surges through
    All times and worlds, nature and humankind?
    O Light of light, such spirits are not blind
To thy perfections, old yet ever new !
    When speech but mocks the overburdened heart,
    They, choosing silence, choose the better part.

April 12, 1883.

# THE RISE OF MAN.

THOU for whose birth the whole creation yearned
   Through countless ages of the morning world,
  Who, first in fiery vapors dimly hurled,
Next to the senseless crystal slowly turned,
  Then to the plant which grew to something more, —
Humblest of creatures that draw breath of life, —
Wherefrom through infinites of patient pain
  Came conscious man to reason and adore :
Shall we be shamed because such things have been,
  Or bate one jot of our ancestral pride?
  Nay, in thyself art thou not deified
That from such depths thou couldst such summits win?
  While the long way behind is prophecy
  Of those perfections which are yet to be.

March 15, 1883.

# THE MAN JESUS.

TO C. P. G.

I F, where thou art, thou knowest more than I
    Can know, amid these earthly vapors dim,
Of that great Soul, who often, in the days
That are no more, allured our common thought,
And made our homeward talk grow strangely deep
And tender, underneath the quiet stars, —
If there thou knowest I have done him wrong,
Failing in aught to give him reverence due,
Thou wilt forgive, being right well assured
That still for simplest truth my spirit yearns
As in those dear and unforgotten days
When life was sweeter than it e'er can be
Again, until again I am with thee.

1881.

# STARLIGHT.

"LOOK up," she said; and all the heavens blazed
    With countless myriads of quiet stars,
Whereon a moment silently he gazed,
    And drank that peace no trouble ever mars.
Then looking down into her face upturned,
    Two other stars that did outshine the rest
Upward to him with such soft splendor yearned
    That all her secret was at once confessed.
Then he with kisses did put out their light,
    And said, "O strange, but more dear love to me
Are thy pure eyes than all the stars of night
    That shine in heaven everlastingly!
Night still is night, with every star aglow;
But light were night didst thou not love me so."

1878.

# THE GOLDEN WEDDING.

NOVEMBER 8, 1882.

OH, many are the songs of love
   The blessed poets sing !
Fain to your happy meeting, friends,
   Would I some message bring ;
Some song of theirs like marriage bells
   To jubilantly swing.

But when I turn their pages o'er
   And read their honeyed verse,
I find, alas ! this love, which they
   So tenderly rehearse,
Is not the love which time has proved
   For better or for worse.

Theirs is the love of youth and maid,
  With May and June aglow,
Who reck not of the falling leaf
  Nor of November's snow;
Enough for them the joyous hours
  That sweetly come and go.


We need another song to-night,
  This love to celebrate,
Which first began so long ago
  And still, by happy fate,
Has hope of other years to come,
  To bless and consecrate.


The love of youth is warm and sweet,
  But theirs is better far
Who walk together from the dawn
  Till shines the evening star,
As late I saw it shining clear
  Above the horizon's bar.

Fade out the Present's happy scene,
  The laughter and the glow ;
Shine once again the faces dear
  Of fifty years ago ;
And set the merry wedding bells
  A ringing to and fro !

Dear hearts, is there a face that comes
  To bless your golden year
Of all the happy swarm that ringed
  With tenderness and cheer
Your wedding joy, so tremulous
  It seemed almost a fear ?

How few remain ; but God is good,
  And from the dim unknown
How many blessed things have come
  For you to call your own,
For loss of that which might not stay
  To graciously atone !

What joy of children in the house
    To nourish and caress,
And grow with every added year
    In love and faithfulness,
Till children's children gather round
    To honor and to bless.


Not unacquainted have the years
    With various sorrow been ;
Full many a day of tears has come
    The happy days between,
And veiled the brightness of the world
    As with a cloudy screen.


But humble hearts that love aright
    From sorrow as from joy,
Draw out a blessing sweet and pure
    From every base alloy ;
The peace of God which nothing can
    Endanger or annoy.

Now blessings on the happy bride
    Of fifty years ago !
And blessings on the husband fond,
    Who then could little know
What grace of God the hidden times
    Were waiting to bestow !

Better than any hope or dream
    Has been the lengthening way ;
Look back and see the tender lights
    Among the shadows play,
While forward brighter shines the path,
    Till comes the perfect day.

Dear Father, Mother, words are weak
    To prove our kindly will ;
More than we hope in this glad hour
    May God's high grace fulfil,
And all the great immortal years
    But find you lovers still.

# THE GOOD SHIP "REGISTER."

Written for a Celebration of the Sixtieth Anniversary of the founding of the "Christian Register," April, 1881.

THIS is a song of the brave old ship
 That has carried aloft for sixty years
The flag of a country of dateless time,
 The country of all men's hopes and fears,
Of all men's longings on land or sea
For the better things that are yet to be.


New-England built was the ship I sing :
 Never in forest her timbers grew ;
Nay, but in soil where the drenching rain
 And the needful sun and the sparkling dew
Were of that pure essence which only can
Come from the great, deep heart of man.

" Come," said the builders, "and let us make
    Such a ship as never was seen before,
Sharp in the bows and broad in the beam,
    And deep in the hold for the mighty store
Of truth and love which her freight will be,
As she breasts the waves of the stormy sea."

Great was the scorn of the scorners then :
    " Build you as we in the good old way,
Or the time and the storm will come," they cried,
    " When the crew of your ship shall rue the day
When in craft of yours they dared the sea."
But the doom which they promised is yet to be.

For the builders built in the scorners' spite
    After the pattern untried before,
And there came in April a pleasant day
    When they gave the ship from the quiet shore
To the seas that wrestle and tug and strain,
To the boundless sweep of the roaring main.

Long ago was that April day ;

    Many times since then has the year gone round ;

Many a voyage the ship has made ;

    Often outward and inward bound,

The lights that never were known to fail

Have given her greeting or parting hail.


On peaceful errands her sails have filled ;

    News she has carried of joy and peace ;

Souls that have suffered in darkness long

    Have at her coming found glad release ;

And souls in famine and mortal fear

Have read on her pennon "Good cheer ! Good cheer !"


No man of war, but the time has been,

    When, flinging their insolent challenge abroad,

The great three-deckers of ancient wrong

    Have heard her thunder for man and God,

And felt her answer of rattling hail

Beat on their decks like an iron flail.

Best she has loved the common way
  Of the great high seas, where a thousand ships
Freighted with simplest loves and cares
  Sail where the wide horizon dips
To friendly shores, and to havens calm,
And to islands breathing an air of balm.


But when she has heard of the ships that have gone
  Sounding a dim and perilous way,
Seeking a land that is still unknown,
  Where the light is not of our common day,
Stranger than seas of the frozen pole,
The infinite vast of the human soul, —


Then she has said, in her Captain's voice,
  "Why do we always tarry here,
Keeping the dear familiar ways,
  Hearing the voices of homely cheer?
Tempt we, good vessel, the unknown sea,
And learn of its tidings, whatever they be."

So many a time she has steered her way
  Far remote from the beaten track,
Sounding and searching for many a day,
  But ever bringing one message back :
" Much have we learned on our voyage lone,
But we have not fathomed the great Unknown."

Tried and true have her Captains been, —
  The brave old ship's that has sailed so long, —
Some of them here we meet no more,
  And some there are whom my foolish song
Will little please, as a landsman's strain
Of things that are done on the open main.

And one there was whom I called my friend, —
  Whom I loved, and I know that he loved me, —
O Mumford, where are you sailing now,
  Across what wonderful, secret sea?
Shall we meet again?   Shall I ever hear
Again your greeting of tenderest cheer?

I give you joy that the good ship flies
 The same old flag of the former days.
I give you joy that her Captain still
 Is a man of the same old simple ways
You loved so well, — a man you knew,
And found him tender and trusty and true.


But now it is time that I make an end :
 Long may the good ship keep the sea !
Ever honest and simple and brave
 May her Captain and all her sailors be !
And ever with gladness all good men hail
The cheerful gleam of her coming sail !

April, 1881.

# ANTI–DISCOURAGEMENT.

THE legend runs, that on his toilsome way
    To reach the Buddha's crown of sacred joy,
Gautama lived a hundred various lives,
    Deeming no task too mean for his employ,

So might he come at length to that high seat
    Which is the topmost sovereignty of good,
And for a thousand ages bless the world
    With the hell-deep salvation of the Buddh.

Of Buddhas there had been before his day
    Twoscore and five ; and when the first of all
Was on this earth, it chanced he came anear
    A hermit's cell, Gautama's, who did fall

Prone on his face, and of his body made

    A living bridge, whereby the teacher crossed

A rushing stream ; and for this service he

    Had gained, instead of that poor life he lost,


At once the Buddha's own ; but " No," he said,

    " I still will go the round of life and death

Some ages more, if so I may at length

    Redeem *all* creatures that draw painful breath."


And of the many forms in which abode

    The spirit which is now the Lord of all,

One was a small red squirrel, and full oft

    Lower than this, for love's sake, did he fall.


And lo ! there came a dreadful storm, which tore

    Gautama's squirrel-nest from off its tree,

And bore it, with its freight of helpless life,

    Far out upon a black and raging sea.

How save his young?   Audacity of love !

   Quoth he, " At length this pretty brush of mine

Shall serve me well, for with it I will dry

   This deep sea up of all its weltering brine."


And so with valiant heart he went to work

   To save his brood ; and seven days he wrought,

Sprinkling the sea on the unconscious land,

   Nor would believe that it was all for naught.


Then Sekra, ruler of the heavens, saw

   What he was at, and laughed right merrily

To think a squirrel, with his tail, should deem

   That he could dry the unfathomable sea.


" Ho, there ! " he cried, " a hundred thousand men

   Could not accomplish what thou dost essay

If they should toil a hundred thousand years,

   And all the hours were years of every day."

" Thou speakest true," the squirrel-saint replied ;
    " So would it be if all were like to thee :
But mind, old imbecile, thine own affairs —
    *I* shall go on till I have dried the sea."


So with new ardor he frisked up and down
    The wild sea's edge, hearing his young ones cry,
Till Sekra ceased to laugh, and, looking down
    With wondering pity from the inclement sky,


That such vast courage could have found a home
    In such a feeble creature's tiny breast,
Soothed all his winds to sleep, and o'er the deep
    Spread suddenly a sweet and perfect rest,


Save where one kindly zephyr gently pressed
    Landward the leafy squirrel-laden bough,
Till there was laughter in the heart which then
    Was a red squirrel's, but is Buddha's now.

O mighty power of love !   O heart that dares

   All things for its beloved !   To you alone

All things are possible ; the heavens bend,

   And powers that scoffed will help you to your own !

1880.

# SEVEN TIMES ELEVEN.

FROM seven times one the tender song went on
    To seven times seven, and there made an end ;
But so, thank God, it has not been with thee
    And thy good years, O dear and blessed friend !

Thy seven times eight had passed ere first I knew
    The kindly welcome of thy pleasant face ;
Thy seven times nine beheld thee full of years,
    But yet more full of gentleness and grace.

Then came the goal, — the threescore years and ten ;
    Still sang thy heart its sweet and natural song :
" Labor and sorrow "?   Nay, to thee I deem
    Labor and joy forevermore belong.

For thou hast ever found thy sweetest joy

    In simple tasks of love and friendliness;

Finding, like one to me forever dear,

    That naught is easier than to cheer and bless.


And so thy *seven times eleven* comes

    And finds thee laboring and loving still;

Striving, ere yet the day is wholly done,

    To fit thy task yet closer to His will.


Work on, love on, in sorrow, yet in joy;

    Another *song of seven* live to sing

Ere, life well spent, thy winter turn at last

    To sudden freshness like this month of spring.


Somehow my lyre is broken in these days,

    Nor makes the music that it made of yore;

But mid the jar this note at least sounds true:

    God's peace be with thee now and evermore!

April 23, 1882.

# JAN STEENER'S RIDE.

A STORY is it, you want, little man?
  Well, come and sit on your grandfather's knee,
And I 'll do the best that ever I can —
  It 's one my grandfather told to me.


Folks think me young for eighty ; well,
  He was almost ninety, and hale and bright,
And I was sitting, as you are now,
  Snug in his arms one winter night.


Said he : " When I was a smart young man —
  Before the Dutch had the country lost —
There stood a church on the village green,
  Right in the middle where two roads crossed.

" It stood as flush with the village street
 As the top o' your head with the palm o' my hand, —
So ; and running from east to west,
 Open each end to the pleasant land,


" Spread out like a picture, the broad aisle ran,
 With the dominie's pulpit a bit one side
Of the upper end ; and there he stood,
 Sounding his trumpet far and wide,


" One Sabbath morning, as pretty a day
 As ever the Lord God chose to make ;
And what do you think was the Bible text
 The dear old dominie chanced to take


" That morning, but one from the 'Pocalypse
 'Bout the great white horse and his rider, Death ?
He was just beginning on ' ninthly,' and
 The people were most of them holding their breath,

" When all at once, in at the open door,
    And up the aisle with a thunderous sound,
Riding as white a horse as a man
    Could find in all the country round,


" There came a horseman galloping fast —
    A single flash — he had come and gone,
Leaving a hundred Dutch-folk there
    With their hearts in their breasts like an icy stone.


" And the dominie he was scared the worst
    Of 'em all; he trembled and shivered and shook,
And gripped the pulpit as if he thought
    The dreadful day of the Holy Book


" Had come for sure ; and at last he said :
    ' What we have seen I dare not say ;
But if it be a sign of the end,
    There is need for us all to watch and pray. '

" So with prayer and blessing the frightened folk
 Were all to their various homes dismissed ;
But one old burgher said, and swore,
 As he shook like a hammer his grimy fist,


" He 'd bet a thousand thalers to one
 That the man who rode and the clattering steed
Were just a younker of flesh and blood
 And a handsome horse of the Flemish breed.


" And, in truth, he was n't much out, my lad !
 I ought to know, for the horse was mine,
And I was the younker that struck aghast
 The dominie preaching his number nine.


" Don't look so solemn !   You see, that day
 I was bound to see the prettiest girl
That ever looked in a looking-glass
 To conquer a wilful and wandering curl.

"And the shortest way to her side was through
   The meeting-house aisle; so through I went.
A minute's difference, more or less;
   But life at the longest will soon be spent,


"And the love of a girl who is sweet and true
   Is a thing so precious beneath the sun
That one of its minutes is worth an age
   Of hearts that never such bliss have won."


This is the story my grandfather told
   To yours; it was fourscore years ago.
That is my grandmother's picture there;
   Do you wonder much that he loved her so?

1875.

# STORM AND SHINE.

## I.

ANOTHER sunless, dreary, weary day !
 How the poor tree-tops shiver ! The dead leaves
Fall sullenly upon the rain-soaked earth ;
 Loud and more loud the wild nor'easter grieves.

And can it be that ever sunlight shone ?
 And can it be that ever skies were blue ?
And can it be that ever breezes soft
 The windward bee scarce hindered as he flew ?

And what if nevermore the earth should lie
 By the warm wind enchanted and caressed ?
And what if this gray shroud which now she wears
 Were that of her last, long, eternal rest ?

## II.

Was ever day so beautiful as this?
    Was ever wind so soft, or sky so fair?
Was ever grass so green, and all the world
    So fresh and pure and sweet beyond compare?

How the glad tree-tops glisten in the sun!
    How, tilting there, the robin flings abroad
A song so gay that all the earth through him
    Seems giving thanks and praises to our God!

And can it be that skies were ever dark?
    That sunlight ever was desired in vain?
That ever fell, day after weary day,
    The hoarded torrents of the cheerless rain?

So beautiful, it seems it cannot die!
    Or die but to bring others to their birth,—
Days fair as this, that with unending joy
    Shall stir the pulses of the happy earth.

# THE MEETING-HOUSE.

"COME," said the fathers, "let us build
    A beacon here beside the sea,
And trim its lamp for those who toss
    On the wide waters wearily."

They built it broad; they built it high;
    They crowned the work with prayer and song;
They set a watchman in the tower
    To tend the light and keep it strong.

Oh, many a frail and wandering bark
    Since then has seen our beacon light,
And hastened home across the dark,
    Rejoicing in the goodly sight!

Long may its starry welcome gleam ;

Long may it guide the weary home ;

Long may its tender message stream

Across the waste of wind and foam !

1879.

# JOHN WEISS.

OVER all the land to-day,
    Where our heroes sleeping lie,
Blooms the amaranthine flower
    That shall never fade or die.

But for us a newer grave
    Flushes with as fair a bloom. —
Bluest of forget-me-nots
    On a stainless soldier's tomb.

He was fellow with them all,
    Wearers of the blue and gray, —
Men who, told that they must die,
    Only asked to know the way.

Ever first in freedom's van,

    Took his breast the sheaf of spears ;

Here is loss too deep for words,

    Here is grief too proud for tears.


Onward, where he led the way !

    Many more will have to fall

Ere the glorious banner waves

    Peace and triumph over all.

DECORATION .DAY, 1879.

# A SONNET FOR THE DAY

FOR WHICH A WEATHER-PROPHET HAD PREDICTED A TERRIFIC
STORM.

A STORM of sunshine ! How it plays and beats
    On the chill gardens and the frozen sods !
How the blue heaven seems as if the gods
Of old with nectarous and ambrosial sweets
Made holiday ! How the very streets,
  Where fashion pours and weary labor plods,
  Seem to laugh out ! What ! Is 't the golden-rod's
Midsummer splendor that my vision greets?
  Nay, 't is the golden sunshine. There is naught
That can withstand its gracious power.
The winter's reign is broken from this hour,
  And all its terrors are to nothing brought.
O heart, my heart, greet thou the opening year,
Sing with the birds and make a sweeter cheer !

March 9, 1883.

# FATE.

ALL unconscious I beheld her;
 Knew not that my fate was nigh, —
Fate that wears such various aspect
 To the victim's laughing eye.

Poets, painters, still to paint her
 Dark and gloomy, do their best;
Were I painter, I would paint her
 All in cherry-color dressed.

She should be a little maiden,
 Modest, shrinking, sweet, and fair,
At a party, playing forfeits,
 Looking, " Kiss me if you dare ! "

Did I kiss you? If I did n't,

'T was the blunder of my life.

Was the last the hundred millionth?

Just one more then, little wife.

January 3, 1880.

.

University Press, Cambridge: John Wilson & Son.

www.ingramcontent.com/pod-product-compliance
Lightning Source LLC
Chambersburg PA
CBHW020804020726
47495CB00008B/2582